Tim Does it Again

by Jan Weeks

illustrated by Janine Dawson

Scholastic Canada Ltd.

Characters

Tim

Mandy

Mom

Contents

Chapter 1

Making Dinner

"I won't be long, Mandy," Mom said. "Take care of Tim. Make sure he doesn't get dirty. We're going out when I come back."

I told Tim that we should watch cartoons.
He didn't want to do that. He wanted to
play outside.

When I went to see what Tim was doing,
he was making mud pies. Tim was using the
hose to turn dirt into mud.

"I'm making them for our dinner, Mandy,"
he said.

Chapter 2

Looking After Tim

Mom was going to be mad when she saw Tim. She was going to be mad with me too. I was supposed to be looking after him.

"Look at you, Tim!" I shouted. "You're filthy. You're covered in mud."

"Don't worry, Mandy," he answered. "It will come off."

Tim wiped his face and hands on the clean sheet on the clothes line.

"Now look what you've done," I gasped. "You got mud all over the sheet."

"It will wash off, Mandy," Tim said. He pulled the sheet from the line. Then he began to drag it through the mud. He was headed for the house.

As he climbed the step, the sheet caught
on a nail. There was a ripping noise. When
I looked, I saw a big tear in the sheet.

My mouth fell open. Things were getting
worse by the second. What was Mom going
to say when she saw that?

Chapter 3

Mandy's Lie

"Look at the sheet, Tim!" I cried. "You've torn a hole in it."

"Don't worry, Mandy," he said. "I can mend it."

"How?" I asked.

"With Wonder-Glue! It's wonderful!" he
gleamed. "Wonder-Glue can fix anything."
Then he looked at me as if I was silly.

I didn't think Wonder-Glue could fix the sheet. I was about to tell him so when the phone rang. I ran into the kitchen to answer it.

It was Mom.

"I'll be home in ten minutes," she said.
"Is everything all right, Mandy?"

"Yes," I lied, feeling guilty.

"I knew I could trust you, Mandy,"
Mom said. Then she hung up.

When I went to find Tim, he had already opened the Wonder-Glue.

"The sheet is stuck to my fingers, Mandy,"
he said. "It won't come off."

"Now what are we going to do?" I groaned.

Chapter 4

Stuck Forever

When I pulled on the sheet, it stayed stuck to Tim's fingers. I pulled harder, but it was no use.

"Is it going to be stuck to me forever, Mandy?" Tim asked. His eyes began to fill with tears.

I had to think of something.

"Maybe we can wash it off," I said, as I
dragged Tim into the bathroom.

I filled the bath with water and dropped
the sheet into it.

Then I told Tim to get in as well.

"With all my clothes on?" he asked.

There was no way to undress him. Not
with a sheet stuck to his fingers!

Putting him in the bath only made things worse. Tim splashed water everywhere as he tried to get the sheet off his fingers.

24

Water went all over the floor. It flowed
out of the bathroom and onto the carpet.

"Now what are we going to do?" Tim asked.

Chapter 5

Caught!

I had a plan. I would get the scissors and cut the sheet off Tim. Then I'd wrap the sheet in newspaper and put it in the garbage.

We could tell Mom that the wind had blown
it away.

It was too late. I had almost finished
cutting when Mom came home.

"Now we're in big trouble," I sighed.

"I wish we hadn't done it," said Tim.

Mom was so angry she sent both of us to our rooms.

I don't think we're ever going to be allowed to come out.

Not for a long time, anyway.

Glossary

filthy
very dirty

gasped
took a short, sharp breath

gleamed
shone

groaned
made a long, low, unhappy sound